Pete the Cat

Cavecat Pete

by James Dean

HARPER

An Imprint of HarperCollins Publishers

Cavecat Pete wakes up early. The sun is shining. The birds are singing.

Today is going to be a great day, Pete thinks. But then Pete's bed starts to shake. His friend Vinny the Velociraptor is coming to visit.

"It's a perfect day for a picnic!" says Vinny.

"What a great idea," says Pete. "Who should we invite?"

"Everyone!" Vinny yells.

"Right on!" says Pete.

Pete loves picnics! He heads out to invite all his friends.

First Pete finds his good friend
Ethel the Apatosaurus!
To get her attention, Pete climbs
all the way up to the top of the
tallest tree.

Pete wanders along the river. He sees T. rex!
T. rex plays guitar. T. rex is awesome!

"Hey, T. rex," Pete yells, "want to come to a picnic?"

"Sweet," says T. rex. "Can I bring my guitar?"

"Definitely," says Pete. "We can jam!"

"Count me in," says T. rex. "Okay if I bring Al the Allosaurus? He's a whiz on the drums."

"The more the merrier," says Pete.

Pete sees his friend Terri the Pterosaur in the sky.
"Hi, Pete!" she calls.

Pete invites Terri to the picnic, too. "Would you
mind giving me a lift?" Pete asks.
"Sure," says Terri. "Climb aboard."

Pete sees the spiked tail of his main man Skip the Stegosaurus.

"How are you feeling today, Skip?" Pete asks. Skip has been sick with the sniffles.

"Better," says Skip. "Thanks for asking."

"You up for a picnic?"

"I think so," says Skip. "I'd hate to miss the fun."

It's almost time for the picnic! Cavecat Pete rushes through the forest. He doesn't want to be late. Whoops! Pete trips over Trini the Triceratops.

"We're playing hide-and-seek," she says before Pete can ask what she was doing. "I think I hid a little too well."

"How long have you been there?" asks Pete.

"What's today?" asks Trini.

"Well, all the dinosaurs are going to be at the picnic grounds. Want to come?" Pete asks.

"What a great idea! Maybe somebody there will play hide-and-seek with me!"

It's time for the picnic. Vinny and Ethel are setting up the picnic tables. T. rex and Al are warming up to play some tunes. Terri and Trini are playing hide-and-seek. Even Skip seems to be enjoying himself!

"It doesn't get any better than this," Pete says.

T. rex comes over then. "Hey, Pete," he asks, "is there anything else to eat? I'm a carnivore. I don't eat salad."

Trini comes over. "Terri is cheating at hide-and-seek. She's flying around and peeking."

Skip comes over. "I don't feel so good," he says, and he sneezes.

The dinosaurs all start to argue. The picnic will be ruined if Pete doesn't do something. He leans over to Al and says, "Can you give me a beat?" Pete takes out his guitar, and he starts to sing.

Before long, everyone is having a great time.
"You know," T. rex tells Ethel, "I've never actually tried salad before."
"Try it," says Pete. "I bet you'll like it."

T. rex tastes the salad. Crunch, crunch, crunch.
"Yum!" says T. rex. "This salad is delicious!"
Everyone grabs a plate and digs in.

Everyone decides to play hide-and-seek. Pete is happy that everyone is getting along. He feels lucky to have such great friends.

"This was the best picnic ever," everyone agrees.

"It was the best picnic because you guys are the best friends ever," Pete says.

And no one can argue with that.